Anonymous

Manual of the First Congregational Church, West Springfield, Mass.

Anatiposi

Anonymous

Manual of the First Congregational Church, West Springfield, Mass.

Reprint of the original, first published in 1858.

1st Edition 2023 | ISBN: 978-3-38231-510-8

Anatiposi Verlag is an imprint of Outlook Verlagsgesellschaft mbH.

Verlag (Publisher): Outlook Verlag GmbH, Zeilweg 44, 60439 Frankfurt, Deutschland
Vertretungsberechtigt (Authorized to represent): E. Roepke, Zeilweg 44, 60439 Frankfurt, Deutschland
Druck (Print): Books on Demand GmbH, In de Tarpen 42, 22848 Norderstedt, Deutschland

MANUAL

OF THE

FIRST CONGREGATIONAL CHURCH,

1st

West Springfield, Mass.,

AND

CATALOGUE

OF

MEMBERS OF THE CHURCH,

SEPTEMBER, 1858.

--⟶∘⟶⦵⟵∘⟵--

NORTHAMPTON:
PRINTED BY METCALF AND COMPANY.
1858.

HISTORICAL RECORD.

The First Congregational Church in West Springfield was organized in June, 1698.

PASTORS.

Names.	Installed.	Removed.
Rev. John Woodbridge,	June, 1698.	Died June, 1718.
" Samuel Hopkins,	June 1, 1720.	" Oct. 5, 1755.
" Joseph Lathrop, D. D.	Aug. 25, 1756.	" Dec. 31, 1820.
" William B. Sprague. D.D.	Aug. 25, 1819.	Dismissed July,1829.
" Tho's E. Vermilye, D. D.	May 6, 1830.	" April 29, 1835.
" John H. Hunter,	Aug. 24, 1835.	" Feb. 16, 1837.
" A. A. Wood, D. D.	Dec. 19, 1838.	" Aug. 28, 1849.
" H. M. Field,	Jan. 29, 1851.	" Nov. 14, 1854.
" T. H. Hawks,	March 7, 1855.	

DEACONS.

Names.	Chosen.	Removed.	
John Barber.	1700.	Died 1712.	Æt. 70.
Ebenezer Parsons.	1700.	" 1752.	" 81.
Joseph Ely.	1712. (?)	" 1755.	" 92.
John Ely.	1712. (?)	" 1758.	" 80.
Samuel Day.	1748.	. " 1773.	" 75.
Joseph Merrick.	1750.	" 1792.	" 88
Nathaniel Atchinson.	1759.	Retired 1782. Died 1801.	" 92.
Jona. White.	1759.	" " " 1805.	" 95.
Pelatiah Bliss.	May, 1782.	Died Oct. 1828.	" 80.
John Bagg.	Feb. 1783.	" June, 1809.	" 78.
Elisha Eldridge.	Sept. 1817.		
Daniel Merrick.	Nov. 1830.	" March, 1855.	" 69.
Horace Smith.	Sept. 1824.		
Edward Southworth.	Nov. 1857.		
Homer Ely.	Nov. 1857.		

Form of Admission

ADOPTED BY THE CHURCH, FEB. 11, 1858.

———— •◦•◦• ————

[*The candidates present themselves as their names are called, and are addressed by the Pastor as follows :*]

YOU are now about to make a public profession of your faith, and to connect *yourselves* with the Church of Christ. We trust you have well considered the nature of this transaction. It is one of the most solemn and important in which you can ever engage. But you come in obedience to Christ; and in humble dependence on Him, you may view it not only as a solemn duty, but a joyful privilege thus openly to connect yourselves with His followers.

You will now give your attention and assent to a brief summary of the System of Doctrines held by this Church.

1*

CONFESSION OF FAITH.

ARTICLE I.

We believe that there is one only, the living and true God, who is revealed to us in the Scriptures as Father, Son, and Holy Ghost, the Maker and Preserver of all things.

II.

That the Scriptures of the Old and New Testaments were given by inspiration of God, and are the only infallible standard of religious doctrine and duty.

III.

That when God created man, He entered into a covenant of life with him, the condition of which was perfect obedience: that man sinned and broke covenant with God by eating the forbidden fruit, and by his disobedience his posterity became sinners.

IV.

That God, of His mere mercy, sent His only-begotten Son into the world, who in our nature has borne the curse of God's law, and brought in everlasting righteousness.

V.

That all who truly believe in Him, are, through His atonement and righteousness, justified from all their sins, and are kept by the power of God, through faith, unto salvation.

VI.

That at the last day, the Lord Jesus Christ will descend from heaven, raise the dead, and judge the world in righteousness: that He will admit His saints to the glory of His kingdom, and punish the ungodly with everlasting destruction.

VII.

That Christ has a kingdom on earth which, in Its visible form, is the Church: that the Sacraments of the Church are Baptism, and the Lord's Supper: that Baptism is to be administered both to believers and their offspring, and that believers in regular Church standing only can consistenly partake of the Lord's Supper.

Do you severally assent to these Articles of Faith?

You will now enter into Covenant with God and with this Church.

THE COVENANT.

In the presence of God and men, you avow the Lord Jehovah to be your God, and the object of your supreme love; the Lord Jesus Christ to be your Saviour; and the Holy Spirit to be your Sanctifier and Comforter.

Confessing the depravity of your hearts, and humbly relying upon divine grace, you promise that you will renounce the ways of sin, and will serve God and Him only, to whom you now solemnly devote yourselves.

You promise that you will diligently observe His commandments and ordinances, in the closet, in the family, and in the sanctuary; and that in all things you will seek the honor of His name and the extension of His kingdom.

You also promise that you will be subject to the government of Christ in this Church: that you will seek its peace and edification, and will faithfully attend upon the ordinances administered in it, endeavoring to grow in grace, and in the knowledge of our Lord and Saviour Jesus Christ.

Do you thus covenant?

[*The ordinance of baptism, if not previously received, is here administered.*]

In view of these your professions and engagements, [*here the Church rise*] we affectionately receive you as members of this Church.

In the name of Christ we welcome you to all the privileges, the labors, and the blessings of the household of Faith : and, on our part, engage to watch over you, and seek your edification so long as you shall continue among us. Should you have occasion to remove, it will be your duty to seek, and ours to grant, a recommendation to some other Church ; for hereafter you cannot withdraw from the watch and communion of the saints without breaking your solemn covenant.

And, now, beloved in the Lord, remember that the vows of God are upon you. They will remain upon you through life, in death, and for ever. Nor is this to you an unwelcome thought. You rejoice rather in the permanency of these sacred and precious bonds. Remember, too, that hereafter the eyes of the world will be upon you : and as you conduct yourselves, the cause of Christ will be honored or dishonored. Let, then, your light so shine before men, that they may see your good works, and glorify your Father which is in heaven. We rejoice that you have been led by the grace of God, as we trust, to this confession of the name of Jesus. Our joy will be permanent, if you continue steadfast in faith, and in the love which is in Christ.

May the Lord support and guide you through this transitory life ; and when its warfare is accomplished, bring us all together into that blessed Church where our communion shall be forever perfect, and our joy forever full! AMEN.

RECEPTION OF MEMBERS FROM OTHER CHURCHES.

[*On the Communion Sabbath, immediately after the admission of those who are received upon profession of their faith,—or, if there are none thus admitted, at the time appropriated to that service,—those who join on certificate rise in their places, as their names are called, and are addressed in the following manner :*]

As you have heretofore made a public profession of your faith, and have been recommended to our fellowship by the Churches to which you have belonged, it is only necessary, at this time, that you assent to the Articles of Faith received by this Church, and do also bind *yourselves* by covenant, to watch over us in the Lord, to seek our purity, peace and edification, and to submit to the government and discipline of Christ as here administered.

Do you thus severally assent and covenant ?

We do, therefore, affectionately receive you as members of this Church, and declare you entitled to all its privileges : and, on our part, engage to watch over you and seek your edification, so long as you shall continue among us. And may the God of all grace make you and us faithful unto death, and minister to us abundantly an entrance into His everlasting kingdom. AMEN.

BAPTISM OF CHILDREN.

———•••———

[Parents in the Church should, without unnecessary delay, present their children for baptism. The time for this service is, ordinarily, the afternoon of the Sabbath following the Communion: and the ordinance is administered immediately after the introductory singing. In special cases, other times may be appointed, concerning which a previous arrangement must be made with the Pastor.]

After the reading of selections from the Scriptures, the child is brought forward, a few appropriate words are chanted, or sung, and the parents assent to the following

BAPTISMAL COVENANT.

Presenting *this child* for Baptism, you profess your belief that in the Covenant of grace, under the Christian dispensation, the offspring of believers are included; that "the promise is unto you and to your children;" that you may commit them to Him who said, "Suffer the little children, and forbid them not, to come unto me; for of such is the kingdom of heaven." And now trusting in the exceeding great and precious promises of God, you do unreservedly dedicate *this child* to His service and glory.

You also place *him* under the watch and care of this Church, claiming for *him* the enjoyment of its privileges and means of grace : and you solemnly engage to strive continually by earnest prayer, by faithful teaching, and by a consistent Christian example, to prepare *him* for full admission to the Church on earth, and the Church triumphant in heaven.

Do you thus profess and engage?

The child is here baptized, a written statement having been previously handed to the Pastor, *of its name, the date of its birth, and the names of both its Parents.*

Church Regulations,

ADOPTED FEB. 11th, 1858.

I. CHURCH MEETINGS.

1. All meetings shall be opened with prayer.

2. All meetings of this Church for the transaction of business, shall be notified on the Sabbath preceding, by the Pastor, or when the office is vacant, by the Clerk, at the request of five members of the Church.

3. There shall be an Annual Meeting on the afternoon of the Thursday immediately following the first Sunday in January, for the review of the preceding year.

At this Meeting, reports shall be made; (1) by the Clerk, respecting additions to and removals from the Church, baptisms, and the residence of absent members; (2) by the Treasurer, respecting the contributions of the Church and Congregation to objects of Christian benevolence; (3) by a Committee consisting of the Superintendent and Assistant Superintendent of the Sabbath School, respecting the religious instruction of the young; (4) by the Standing Committee, respecting the state of religion in the Church and Congregation.

4. An Annual Meeting for business shall be held on the second Tuesday of April, at which the Officers for the ensuing year, except Deacons, shall be elected; the Deacons, Treasurer, and Superintendent of the Sabbath School shall make reports as prescribed in the Articles defining their duties; and such other business shall be done as may be appointed or proper for said meeting.

2

II. OFFICERS.

1. The Officers of this Church shall be a Pastor, four Deacons, a Standing Committee, Clerk, Treasurer, and Superintendent of the Sabbath School.

2. The Pastor shall be chosen according to established precedents, and shall be, ex officio, Moderator of the meetings of the Church, and of the Standing Committee.

3. The Deacons shall be chosen by ballot, and shall hold their office as long as they are acceptable to the Church.

4. All other officers shall be chosen at the Annual Meeting for business, for a term of one year; and they shall be elected by ballot, unless the Church shall otherwise direct.

5. It shall be the particular duty of the Deacons to assist in the administration of the Lord's Supper; to distribute the charities of the Church; and to aid the Pastor generally in the spiritual care of the flock.

6. The Standing Committee shall consist of the Pastor and Deacons, together with three other members of the Church, whose duty shall be to examine candidates for admission to the Church; to attend to matters of discipline, and bring before the Church such cases as, in their judgment, may require its action, and to do whatever business may be referred to them by the Church.

Meetings for the examination of candidates shall be held at such times as the Committee may direct, notice being given from the pulpit on the Sabbath.

7. It shall be the duty of the Clerk to keep a Record containing minutes of the doings of the Church: its Standing Regulations in a place by themselves; a chronological list of its members, with the time of their admission, dismission, death,

&c. so far as he can ascertain the same: also a chronological list of the children presented in Baptism by their parents, recording the name of the child, and of its parents, and the date of its birth. He shall also notify all members who may have been absent more than *nine months*, of their duty to remove their relationship to another church.

8. The Treasurer shall receive all moneys collected, (except the contributions of the Sabbath School,) and shall disburse them for the objects for which they were collected; and at the expiration of his office, shall render a written account of moneys received or expended by him during the preceding year, stating the time of their collection and expenditure, and the objects for which they were expended; which report is to be placed on file by the Clerk.

9. The Superintendent of the Sabbath School, at the expiration of his office, shall render a report in regard to the state of the School during the past year, giving the amount of contributions, for what purpose, and how expended; also presenting any other topics of interest in connection with the School.

III. ORDINANCES.

1. The Sacrament of the Lord's Supper shall be observed the first Sabbath in January, March, May, July, September and November: and the Baptism of children ordinarily on the afternoon of the Sabbath immediately following the Communion.

IV. ADMISSIONS.

1. Persons wishing to unite with this Church on profession of faith, must be examined and propounded, at least two weeks before their public reception.

2. Persons with letters of recommendation from other churches, shall be propounded two weeks before their reception; and they shall be received on the day of, and previous to, the Communion Service, upon their publicly assenting to the Confession of Faith, and the Covenant of the Church.

V. Dismissions.

1. Requests for letters of dismission and recommendation to other churches must, in all cases, be presented to the Church one Sabbath before that on which the vote is taken.

2. No individual can cease to be a member of this Church, unless regularly dismissed and recommended to some other church, or excommunicated for some offense.

VI. Absent Members.

1. Whenever members of this Church shall change their place of residence or worship, it shall be their duty to apply to the Church for letters of dismission and recommendation to some other Church in fellowship with us, if there be such in their neighborhood; and if they shall delay this application more than one year after such change, letters shall not be granted, unless satisfactory reasons are assigned for the delay.

VII. Members of other Churches.

1. No member of another Church, residing among us and accustomed to worship with us, shall be allowed to commune with this Church more than one year, without applying to the Pastor, or other members of the Standing Committee, for admission to the Church, or making known satisfactory reasons for delay.

2. Previous to the administration of the Lord's Supper, a general invitation shall be given to the members of evangelical churches in good standing, to commune with us in that ordinance.

VIII. Discipline.

1. No complaint or information on the subject of a personal or private offense, shall be admitted by the Church, unless the means of reconciliation, or of privately reclaiming the offender, have been used, which are required by Christ, (Matt. xviii: 15, 16,) and in case of a public offense, the same steps shall be taken, when circumstances shall admit.

When a member is accused before the Church, he or she shall be seasonably furnished, by the Clerk, with a copy of the charges, and shall have a full hearing.

While the trial is pending, the accused is expected to abstain from partaking of the Lord's Supper.

2. Individuals under censure may be debarred from the Communion of the Lord's Supper during any period the Church may think proper.

3. Admonition and excommunication are to be administered by the Pastor, or when he is absent, by the Moderator, by a vote of the Church.

IX. Obligations.

1. The Church shall feel especially bound to take a general charge of the Sabbath School, and elect its officers, and examine its concerns.

2. The members of this Church feel themselves required by the spirit of the gospel, to abstain from buying, selling, or using, as a beverage, alcoholic drinks, except in case of bodily hurt, infirmity, or sickness.

3. The members of the Church shall be held bound by their covenant, cheerfully to do their part towards supporting the ordinances of the Gospel, in such manner as the Church shall direct.

X. Benevolent Societies.

1. We recognize the following Societies as the principal channels of our contributions :—American Bible Society, American B. C. F. Missions, American Tract Society, Mass. Sabbath School Society, Seamen's Friend Society, American Home Missionary Society, American Education Society, American Foreign and Christian Union.

2. Collections may be made at such times, and in such a manner, as the Standing Committee may direct.

XI. Religious Services.

1. Besides the usual Sabbath services,—Monthly Concert of Prayer for Missions, on the first Sabbath evening of each month.

2. Sabbath School Concert, second Sabbath evening of each month.

3. Church Prayer Meeting on Thursday evening of each week, unless otherwise noticed from the pulpit.

4. Lecture preparatory to the Lord's Supper on Friday afternoon preceding Communion season, unless notice is otherwise given from the pulpit.

XII. Pastoral Vacancy.

1. Whenever this Church and Society are destitute of a settled Pastor, there shall be a Special Committee of three chosen by the Church to act in concert with a Committee to be chosen by the Society, to supply the pulpit until a Pastor shall be settled.

XIII. Amendments.

1. Any of the foregoing Regulations may be amended by a vote of the Church ; the amendment having been read before the Church two weeks previous to acting upon it.

Catalogue of Members,

SEPTEMBER, 1858.

NOTE.—c. signifies that the person was received by certificate from another Church,

w. stands for widow; parentheses include the husband's name.
The date following each name indicates the time of admission.

A.

Alderman, Mrs. Sally, (Talcott.)	
Alley, Henry,	July, 1839.
Alley, Mrs. Mary L. (Henry,)	March, 1839.
Alley, Louisa Caroline,	May, 1851.
Ashley, Mrs. Caroline, w.(Solomon,)	June, 1795.
Ashley, Mrs. Sybil, w. (Enoch,)	June, 1818.
Ashley, Moses,	July, 1839.
Ashley, Joseph,	1822.
Ashley, Mrs. Elizabeth, (Joseph,)	1829.
Ashley, Elizabeth S.	Jan. 1856.
Ashley, Annah,	Sept. 1855.
Ashley, Mrs. Julia, (Ebenezer,)	1824.
Ashley, Mrs. Lydia, w. (Francis,)	1824.
Ashley, Chauncey,	July, 1839.
Ashley, Mrs. Emily F. (Chauncey,)	Sept. 1855.
Ashley, Martin,	July, 1839.
Ashley, Sophronia,	1819.
Ashley, Charlotte E.	Jan. 1856.

B.

Bagg, Richard, Oct. 1815.

Bagg, Mrs. Flavia, (Richard,) Oct. 1815.

Bagg, Mrs. Susan A. w. (Richard, Jr.) Nov. 1842.

Bagg, Aaron, May, 1839.

c. Bagg, Mrs. Lucy, (Aaron,) Nov. 1838.

Bagg, Lucy Maria, • Nov. 1855.

Bagg, James, Oct. 1815.

c. Bagg, Mrs. Sybil, (James,) July, 1810.

Bagg, J. Newton, July, 1839.

c. Bagg, Mrs. Fanny, w. (Linus,) Sept. 1813.

Bagg, Mrs. Sophia, (Abram,) July, 1839.

Bagg, Mrs. Catharine, (Charles,) May, 1841.

c. Bagg, Ralph, May, 1845.

c. Bagg, Mrs. Lurana, (Ralph,) May, 1845.

c. Bagg, Ebenezer, May, 1857.

c. Bagg, Mrs. Theda M. (Ebenezer,) May, 1857.

Bagg, Mrs. Persis E. (Gilbert,) Nov. 1855.

Bagg, Helen M. Sept. 1855.

Beals, Mrs. Mary B. (Lorin,) May, 1839.

Beebe, Mrs. Elizabeth, w. (Richard,) Sept. 1835.

Beebe, Eliza, • 1823.

Belden, Mrs. Lucy B. E. w. (Chauncey,) Jan. 1840.

Bellows, Horace Edward, Sept. 1858.

c. Bliss, Mrs. Susannah, w. (Jeduthan,) May, 1806.

Bliss, Jeduthan, July, 1836.

Bliss, Mrs. Lucretia, (Jenubath,) Nov. 1815.

Bliss, Mrs. Lucy, w. (Elijah,) Nov. 1808.

Bliss, Mrs. Ann, (Caleb,) Jan. 1837.

Bliss, Charles Henry, Sept. 1839.

c. Bliss, Mrs. Eunice D. w. (Gad,) July, 1846.

Bliss, Mrs. Eunice D. (Rev. Isaac,) Nov. 1841.
Bliss, Tirzah, Nov. 1843.
Bliss, Sophia, March, 1839.
Bliss, Sarah, Jan. 1856.
Bosworth, Zadock.
Bosworth, Mrs. Julia, (Zadock.)
Bosworth, Alonzo, July, 1839.
c. Bosworth, Mrs. Mary S. (Alonzo,) Sept. 1850.
Bosworth, Julia Ann, Nov. 1848.
Bosworth, Lucy Maria, May, 1851.
c. Brooks, Mrs. Angeline, (Jonathan,) June, 1824.
Brooks, Angeline, Sept. 1855.
Brooks, Ethan, Nov. 1847.
Brooks, Mrs. Hannah, (Ethan,) March, 1851.
Brooks, Eliab, 1824.
c. Brooks, Philo, Sept. 1852.
Brooks, Eliza A. Nov. 1855.
c. Burns, Mrs. Mary, w. (John,) July, 1841.
Bush, Orel, Oct. 1815.

C.

Champion, Flavia, 1824.
Chapin, Joseph C. Sept. 1839.
Chapin, Mrs. M. Marytta, (Joseph.) Sept. 1842.
Clark, Anson K. 1826.
Clark, Mrs. Laura, (Anson K.) 1826.
c. Colton, Rufus, July, 1851.
c. Colton, Mrs. Lucretia, (Rufus,) July, 1851.
Colton, Benjamin, Nov. 1816.
c. Colton, Mrs. Eliza, (Benjamin,) July, 1839.
Colton, Betsey, March, 1848.

Cooley, Mrs. Lorinda, w. (Charles,)   1819.
Cooley, Mrs. Sarah, (Walter,)   Nov. 1831.
Cooley, Rev. Henry,   1828.
Cooley, Lucy,   March, 1839.
Cooley, Polly,   1824.
Cooper, Mrs. Mary, (Josiah,)   Nov. 1834.
c. Craige, Mrs. Martha, w.   Sept. 1856.

D.

Day, Aaron,   April, 1811.
Day, Mrs. Anna, (Aaron,)   April, 1811.
Day, Lucinda,   1824.
c. Day, Lydia E.   March, 1853.
c. Day, Mrs. Deborah B. w. (Plin,)   Jan. 1842.
c. Day, Sherebiah B.   Sept. 1839.
c. Day, Mrs. Harriet, (Sherebiah,)   Sept. 1839.
Day, Harriet,   Sept. 1855.
Day, Mrs. Elizabeth, w. (Daniel,)   Jan. 1807.
Day, Norman,   July, 1839.
Day, Mrs. Aurelia, (Norman,)   July, 1836.
Day, Mrs. Lovisa, w. (Rodney,)   Nov. 1808.
Day, Mrs. Susan, w. (Heman,)   May, 1843.
Day, Frances,   May, 1839.
Day, Lois Ann,   July, 1851.
Dorne, Gilman A.   Sept. 1858.
c. Downes, Nathaniel,   July, 1851.
Downes, Mrs. Ann Maria, (Nathaniel,) Nov. 1855.
Dwight, Mrs. Olive, w. (Abiel,)   1819.

E.

Efner, Mrs. Sophia W. (Henry,)   May, 1848.
Eldridge, Dea. Elisha,   May, 1812.

Eldridge, Mrs. Tryphena, (Elisha,) Sept. 1815.
Eldridge, James D.   May, 1839.
c. Eldridge, Mrs. Sarah, (James D.)   Aug. 1846.
c. Eldridge, Mrs. Eliza, (Oliver,)   Aug. 1846.
Eldridge, Lora A.   May, 1849.
c. Ely, Mrs. Abigail, w. (Justin,)   April, 1809.
Ely, Mrs. Nancy L. (Justin,)   1823.
Ely, Dea. Homer,   Jan. 1816.
Ely, Mrs. Anna, (Homer,)   Jan. 1816.
Ely, Homer, Jr.   July, 1858.
Ely, Maria N. (Homer, Jr.)   July, 1858.
Ely, Celia S.   July, 1855.
Ely, Cotton,   1824.
Ely, Mrs. Marietta, (Cotton,)   1824.
Ely, Mrs. Anna, (Nathan,)   July, 1803.
Ely, James P.   July, 1841.
Ely, Mrs. Mercy, (James P.)   July, 1841.
c. Ely, Mrs. Orpha, (Pelatiah,)   Dec. 1845.
Evans, Jane,   May, 1851.

F.

Fenn, Mrs. Augusta B.   March, 1848.
Fox, Mrs. Sarah E. (Charles,)   July, 1858.

G.

Goff, Betsey,   Sept. 1831.
Griggs, Mrs. Elvira, (Solomon,)   May, 1839.

H.

Harmon, Eliza Jane,   Nov. 1857.
Hathaway, Henry,   July, 1855.
c. Hawks, Mrs. Mary H. (Rev. T. H.) Nov. 1855.

Hitchcock, Mrs. Frances A. (Dexter,) Jan. 1856.
Humeston, Louisa L. 1824.

J.

c. Jones, William, Sept. 1856.
c. Jones, Mrs. Melinda, (William,) Sept. 1856.
Jones, Mrs. Maria B. (Philip,) May, 1839.

K.

Kent, Elizabeth, Nov. 1837.

L.

Lathrop, Mrs. Lora, w. (Dwight,) Oct. 1807.
c. Leonard, James, March. 1852.
c. Leonard, Mrs. Mary, (James,) March. 1852.
Leonard, Lewis, July, 1839.
Loomis, Mrs. Dinah, (Ely,) May, 1858.
Lloyd, Isaac H. May, 1856.
c. Lloyd, Mrs. Sarah G. (Isaac,) May, 1856.
Lyman, Elias C. July, 1855.

M.

Merrick, Mrs. Laura, w. (Dea. Daniel,) 1824.
Merrick, Joseph, July, 1839.
Merrick, Charles, Nov. 1847.
Miller, Asa, Sept. 1831.
Miller, Mrs. Laura, (Asa,) 1824.
Miller, Joel, Jr. July, 1858.
Miller, Mrs. Mary C. (Joel, Jr.) July, 1839.
Miller, Ellen S. Nov. 1856.
Morgan, Mrs. Fanny, w. (Nathan,) 1823.

Morgan, Elizabeth,	Sept. 1855.
Morgan, Justin,	July, 1839.
Morgan, Lester,	May, 1839.
Morgan, Samuel,	May, 1839.
Morgan, Roxanna,	Sept. 1817.
c. Moseley, Mrs. Jane S. (J. O.)	July, 1839.

P.

Palmer, Mrs. Sabra, w. (Henry,)	Dec. 1811.
Parsons, Edward,	1822.
Parsons, Mrs. Sophronia, (Edward,)	May, 1839.
Parsons, Martha,	July, 1839.
c. Parsons, Carlos,	Sept. 1857.
c. Parsons, Mrs. Elizabeth, (Carlos.)	Sept. 1857.
Phelps, Mrs. Lucinda, (Moses,)	Jan. 1858.
Philips, Sarah Ann,	May, 1856.

R.

Reed, Edwin W.	July, 1858.
Reed, Martha Isabella,	July, 1858.
Rice, Mrs. Roxanna, w. (Morris.)	July, 1858.
c. Richards, William H.	Sept. 1858.
c. Richards, Mrs. Phebe A. (Wm. H.)	Sept. 1858.
Rogers, Mrs. Fidelia S. w. (Ely,)	Sept. 1840.
Root, Mrs. Theodosia, w. (Edward.)	May, 1817.
c. Root, Orrin,	June, 1840.
c. Root, Mrs. Sarah K. (Orrin,)	June, 1840.
Root, Aruma C.	Nov. 1856.
Russell, Mrs. Lauraette,	July, 1858.

s.

c.	Sampson, Ruth G.	Jan. 1856.
	Shaw, Mrs. Maria P.	July, 1839.
	Smith, Dea. Horace,	Sept. 1815.
	Smith, Mrs. Grata. (Horace,)	Oct. 1815.
	Smith, Rev. Henry B.	Jan. 1834.
	Smith, Franklin,	July, 1839.
c.	Smith, Mrs. Sarah F. (Franklin,)	Sept. 1848.
	Smith, Joseph,	July, 1839.
c.	Smith, Frances O. (Joseph,)	Nov. 1848.
	Smith, William H.	Sept. 1847.
c.	Smith, Mrs. Maria L. (William,)	Sept. 1857.
	Smith, Samuel D.	Sept. 1847.
c.	Smith, Mrs. Mary Jane, (Samuel D.)	Jan. 1856.
	Smith, Caroline T.	May, 1851.
c.	Smith, Samuel,	May, 1855.
c.	Smith, Mrs. Ellen L. (Samuel,)	Sept. 1858.
	Smith, Mrs. Anna, w. (Rodolphus,)	1824.
	Smith, Ann,	July, 1839.
	Smith, Mrs. Lucy, w. (Enoch N.)	March, 1842.
	Smith, Lucy E.	July 1858.
	Smith, Mrs. Mary, w. (Noadiah,)	July, 1841.
	Smith, Harvey,	March, 1816.
	Smith, Mrs. Sally, (Harvey,)	1823.
	Smith, Justus,	1819.
	Smith, Mrs. Lydia, (Justus,)	1819.
	Smith, John D.	May, 1839.
	Smith, Rhoda,	May, 1841.
	Smith, Sally,	May, 1842.
	Smith, Daniel,	July, 1839.

c. Smith, Mrs. Anna Maria, (Daniel,) Nov. 1846.
c. Southworth, Dea. Edward,   Dec. 1840.
c. Sykes, Hannah,   Sept. 1858.

T.

Taylor, Mrs. Delight, w. (Henry,)   1819.
Taylor, John B.   July, 1841.
Taylor, William,   May, 1858.
Taylor, Mrs. Martha, (William,)   May, 1858.

U.

Ufford, Mrs. Mary Ann, (Edward,) March, 1851.

W.

c. Wallace, James,   July, 1858.
White, Priscilla,   April, 1809.
White, Daniel G.   May, 1839.
White, Mrs. Harriet, (Daniel,)   May, 1839.
White, Harriet,   Nov. 1855.
White, Henry,   Jan. 1854.
Williams, Lester,   1823.
Williams, Mrs. Cynthia, (Lester,)   1823.
Williams, Ellen S.   Sept. 1852.
Williams, Samuel P.   Nov. 1855.